HONEYMOON ROMANCE

Written by Michael Bryant

TABLE OF CONTENTS

SYNOPSIS

The story starts with Aidan, our protagonist, and his newlywed wife, Elisa, talking in the airplane. They were close to landing. And when they finally land Elisa's future love interest Kai welcomes them. On the way to the hotel Aidan falls asleep.

When They arrive, Elisa wakes him up. As she takes the key from the reception, Aidan slowly spirals down in disturbing thoughts of his wife cheating on him. They get to the room and as Aidan looks around Elisa undresses, surprising Aidan.

Aidan tries to unbutton his shirt, but Elisa stops him. He understands that she wants to be in charge. They have very intimate moments.

The next day both their bodies were covered in small love marks. Kai picks them up in the morning for a city tour. Aidan sees Kai and Elisa very intimate throughout the day. When they sat for lunch, they have a brief conversation, where Aidan learns Kai's major which is the same with Elisa's.

After this Aidan thinks about how he is not in love anymore. When Kai asks him questions Elisa answers in his place and excludes him from the conversation. With this Aidan starts reading his book which has gay characters. It reveals that Aidan had kissed a man before.

After lunch they decide to go around individually. Aidan goes back to the hotel but forget that Elisa had the keys. When Elisa comes back Aidan first thinks that she cheated on him with Kai. When Aidan manages to go back to the room, they have rough sex. Aidan pushes her boundaries to numb his pain.

Aidan was on the beach when he meets Alex. He starts a conversation about his book. Elisa gets jealous over this and says that she is going to the room. Aidan does not go with her. Instead, he goes to grab a lunch with Alex where he learns he has a lot in common with him. Before he went back to his room Alex tells him his door number. When he is back at the room, he and Alisa have a fight and Aidan leaves.

He finds himself standing before Alex's room. Before he can knock the door opens and Alex pulls him in. They have sex. Then Aidan falls asleep.

He has a nightmare where he sees memories flash and his father slowly rotting on one side. When he wakes up Alex was his side. Before leaving the room, Aidan gives Alex his number and says to himself that he needs a divorce as soon as possible.

He gets to an empty room. He sits down to write down pros and cons of divorce. Then Elisa comes in with Kai behind him. He leaves when he sees Aidan. When the two were left alone they have a confrontation. Elisa leaves the room with her belongings

Next time Aidan sees her is at the airport while she signs the divorce papers.

Two years passes and Aidan is a Linguist at MIT. Out of nowhere William comes along and they decide have dinner at Aidan's place. After this Aidan remembers why he never stayed in touch with him.

They have a nice dinner, then they start to drink. William gets drunk and they have sex. Aidan imagines Alex but does not climax. He takes a shower but when he is back William is already asleep. Next morning William questions Aidan about Alex. They have sex again to numb Aidan's pain. William stays for a week at Aidan's place. After he is gone Aidan gets worse.

One day before class he sees a familiar flash of ginger. He turns around to find Alex. They hug each other. And Alex gives Aidan an address for dinner.

When Aidan arrives at the place, he sees that the place is rented for the whole night by some stranger. He sits on the pavement and waits for Alex.

When Alex arrives, he tells him the situation only to learn that the stranger who rented the place was Alex. They have a very romantic dinner and take the dessert for home. They get to Aidan's place and have sex in the kitchen. After that They eat the dessert, and this time Alex carries Aidan to the bedroom and have sex there. Before Aidan falls asleep, he sees a glimpse of his father and whispers that he will not pay like he did.

CHAPTER 1

It was a lovely sight from the airplane. The small islands of the Caribbean were sprinkled all over the endless ocean. As we descended, I started to see the silhouettes of buildings standing afar. I was excited. This was our honeymoon. After all the struggles we went through, we had made it. We. Were. Married.

I looked at *my* stunning Elisa. She was reading her favorite book, Outlander. I did not know how come she was reading it for the third time without getting bored. There was no sign of monotony on her face when she turned to me and smiled.

"What is it, love?" she asked.

"I am just amazed that you're still reading Outlander after all these years," I answered.

She shrugged, "Well, I love the story." and added, her voice was filled with sarcasm, "And I was reading it when we first met. I wanted to feel the nostalgia,"

I grinned, "I'll show you nostalgia when we get to the hotel," I kissed her.

It was a grim fact that we were not able to find time to have intimacy for the last two years. I was in Japan for my job, and we continued our relationship long distance. I had missed feeling her, making her beg for more. I always loved the way she arched her back when she was about to reach climax. It was a sight to see.

We remained quiet for the rest of the flight. The changing landscape from the window indicated the arrival. We waited for most of the people to leave before rising from our seats. I knew Elisa thought planes were busses for the rich. She was not totally wrong. It always took a tremendous amount of time for people to get their cabin baggage.

After an hour or so, we were able to get our luggage. We walked past the last pair of doors into the incoming passenger. Our tour guy was already there.

"Hello," he said, "I am Kai Jonathan Wilson. I will be guiding you during your vacation."

He shook both our hands. Elisa had already started to ask questions by the time we reached the vehicle provided for us.

I closed my eyes and leaned back. My wife's soothing voice echoed as I fell asleep.

***

I woke up with the gentle touch of Elisa. We had arrived at the hotel.

"I will see you tomorrow morning for our city tour. Until then take care," He kissed Elisa's hand, and shook mine. I looked at him closely as he walked out of the hotel. He was a charming mid-twenties man. He was a little taller than I was, and his skin was looked like chocolate. He had curly black hair. His body had the right amount of muscle.

I shook my head, intending to get rid of the disturbing thoughts. I looked at Elisa. She was taking the keys from the receptionist with a smile.

When our eyes meet, her smile turned into a dirty grin, and I knew what that meant.

Our room was small, but it was enough. It had a double bed, a mini fridge, a table and a TV unit. I walked to the window and looked out.

"Well, at least we have a nice view," I turned to face Elisa.

I swallowed hard with the sight of her naked body.

"W-when did you undress?" I asked. She walked up to me and drew the blinds.

I reached up my collar to unbutton, but she stopped me. She pressed her body to mine and kissed me instead. That is how I understood she wanted to be in charge. Her tongue discovered inside my mouth soon enough. I tasted the honey she ate on the plane. I parted from her.

"You taste sweet," I murmured, my eyes closed.

She did not answer. Instead, she moved her lips to my jaw, traced my jawline with her tongue, and when she reached my neck, she started marking her territory. I was quite sure she had left small bruises already. I moaned when she bit my collarbone. My head fell back in pleasure, and my mouth gaped. She started unbuttoning my shirt. She was slow, agonizingly slow. But I knew better than to interrupt her. When she was done with buttons, she pushed the shirt back and started kissing my torso—tracing her way down to my stiff penis.

She knew me way too well. So, she undid my jeans with her mouth. Her teeth gently pulling my jeans down was a sight that could make any man go mad. I groaned and pushed my hips towards her. She pulled my boxer down and took my penis into her hands. Stroking it gently, she started to kiss the tip of it. I looked at her. She was so beautiful. The way she looked at me when she was down on her knees was perfection.

She took the whole length in her mouth, making it hit her throat. I was caught off guard and moaned loudly. She gaged on my penis. When she took it out, spit was dripping from the corners of her mouth. I looked at her, begging with my eyes. She nodded and started to move her mouth around my penis.

This was our special bond. The way we managed to communicate without words. She knew me, and I knew her. She tortured me for what felt like hours—pulling away when I got close, and then wrapping her tongue around me again when I calmed down. When she finally took me to bed, I was a mess.

She laid on the bed and spread her legs. She was shameless, and I loved that. She expected me to take her right away, but I had a different idea.

I lowered my body. My face was facing between her legs. Kissing and licking, I started to drive her insane. She was soaking wet already, and she probably was ready. I was not going to show her any mercy, though. I kept going like that for a while. I stopped when she was a moaning mess, like I was when it was her turn to torture.

When I felt like she was close, I positioned myself to her. When I slid inside her, we both moaned. It had been so long, and she was tight like always. I started moving. She cried my name. I got faster, and it felt too good. Soon after, I felt her tightening around me. We both reached climax, moaning each other's names.

"Well, that was nostalgic," I said, when I caught my breath.

"Yes, it was better than old times, though," Elisa laughed.

I looked at her. Her naked body looked as if it belonged to a goddess. She was the definition of perfection in my eyes.

"You're so perfect," I murmured softly. Elisa looked at me and gave me a half-smile.

I kissed her. I knew what we just had was the beginning of something much more.

CHAPTER 2

The next day both our bodies were sore and covered in small bruises. Love marks left on our skins after a sweet, long night.

Kai had picked us up at 8 am for the city tour. It was not any different from most cities, I thought. But Elisa loved city photography. The entire day, we were surrounded by cement color buildings. Everything was grey in this city. Not that I do not like grey. It was a beautiful color. It was the color of the unknown.

Throughout the day, I saw multiple occasions where Elisa and Kai were intimate. Kai would put his hand on Elisa's arm to show her a gorgeous frame to shoot, and Elisa would squeak like a happy hamster. It was getting annoying. I was not the jealous type, but even I could feel the attraction between them.

"So, Kai," I started, "Are you married?"

"What! No, marriage isn't my thing, you see?" he answered.

"But you must have a girlfriend, for sure?" I tried again, only to release the pain within me. I hoped to have a definite answer.

"Nope," he said, crushing my hopes.

"Well, that's unfortunate," said Elisa, she was grinning.

"Not really," explained Kai, "You see, I am studying on my master's degree, and with this job and schoolwork, I have only time for one-night stands." He laughed charmingly.

"How interesting. What are you mastering on?" asked Elisa, her eyes were visibly darkened with lust.

"English Literature," simply answered Kai.

Shit. It was Elisa's major. After this answer, they started to talk about who was the best poet in the Victorian era. Kai said Bryon,

Elisa was stunned. They had a lot in common. I did not, so sank into my thoughts.

I remembered moments of happiness, the beginning of our relationship. Elisa used to be my heavenly sanctuary. She used to be. Now she was nothing more than a woman I liked to have company at night. But of course, there was no way I could tell her this. It would crush her. So, I let the weight of the lies break me instead.

My mother had always said, I was too gentle to tell the truth, and one day this treat of mine would drag me to a disaster. It seemed like it did. It pulled me into a marriage, in which I was lying to my own wife. I chuckled to myself. My wife. Yes, she was my wife, and currently, she was flirting with our tour guy on our honeymoon. I wondered if it was her personality. I could be that she was lying too. I did not know.

We arrived at our carefully selected restaurant by noon. It was buried in the city but looked so out of it. There were tall, green trees on its garden. As we picked a table inside, a waitress came by and got our orders. Kai looked at me.

"What do you like?" he asked.

"Uhm, fantasy and sci-fi literature and race motorbikes," I answered monotonously. There was not much to talk about me except my Lord of the Rings obsession.

"Hmm, which book is your favorite?" he asked.

"Oh, he loves Lord of the Rings," Elisa explained and excluded me from the talk.

I was used to her being the center of any conversation. So, I picked my current book and started reading. It was a way to escape from the pitiful gaze of Kai. The conversation beside me went on, but it was muted. This always happened when I was reading. I came across a sex scene between the main character and the love interest. It was intense. I peeked down at my crotch. No movement.

I was good at controlling my penis as well as my face when it comes to reading erotic scenes.

The main character was male, and so was the love interest, which was a plus. I always liked gay relationships in fiction. I smiled with memories of me and William, my friend from the boarding school I went to. He was also my roommate during college years until I started dating Elisa. I remembered foggy memories of kissing him. I was drunk, of course. I would never make out with a man with a sober mind. I was confused back then. I was simply confused.

I shook my head and kept reading until it muted everything else.

After lunch, we decided to go and explore the city by ourselves. Well, Elise wanted that. So, I took the long road to the hotel. It was a wrong decision.

An hour later, I was sitting on an armchair in the lobby waiting for Elisa. I had forgotten that she had the keys. She came through the door but did not see me. Her shirt was wrinkled, and her hair was messier.

The first thought I had was about Kai. The second was that she loved me enough not to do such a thing. I sat there frozen for another hour before slowly taking the stairs up to the 3rd floor.

When I was in the room, Elisa was sleeping on the bed. I climbed and separated her legs. I slowly took her panties off and started licking. She moaned in her sleep, but soon enough, she woke up. She pushed her hips to my face and groaned.

"Lick harder," I stopped at this, "Please," she begged. I licked harder.

She was asking me to take her, but this time I was in complete charge. And there was no way I had let her go that easy. I licked and sucked and then licked again, until she climaxed. Her back was arched. I kept licking. Slowly she was turning into a mess.

"More, oh, please give me more!" she moaned.

So, I did. I made her reach the highest and watched from above as she came down.

I stood on my knees; my penis erects. She crawled to me. Knowing what I wanted, she opened her mouth. I put it in her mouth and started moving in and out. I was slow at first. Making sure I would go all the way to the end. I made her gag, and as she gaged, I started to increase my pace. I was fast and furious. I knew she thought I was enjoying this. But I did not, I just had to do this. Otherwise, I would ask the unbearable question: Did you cheat on me?

I was not in love with Elisa. Not anymore. But to be cheated on would destroy me. I married her because she was in love with me and basically worshipped in bed. But also, I married her because I knew she would never cheat on me like my mother did on my father. I had seen it. The way she moaned under a stranger in pleasure.

I grabbed Elisa's hair and thrust faster. I wanted to forget. She choked. I needed to forget. She moaned. I knew she liked it. I wondered if she took Kai in like this. I got faster. She choked again. Spit was dripping from her nose and from the corners of her mouth, staining the bedsheets. I had to forget.

I climaxed into her throat with a loud groan. When I pulled out, she coughed. She looked at me through teary eyes. She knew what was on my mind.

"I'm sorry," she whispered.

"Turn around and bend over," I said.

She obeyed quietly. I jerked my penis for a minute before sliding in her. She gave out a painful gasp. I did not care. I was not in the mood to have mercy on her. I needed to get rid of the disturbing thoughts. I thrust hard.

I needed to forget that day.

CHAPTER 3

We were on the beach when I met him. Elisa was swimming. I was not a fan of swimming in open water. I did not feel safe when I was surrounded by fish and other living things. So, I was sitting on my towel and enjoying a good book.

"What are you reading?" an unknown voice asked.

I looked up. There was a man, probably early 20s, standing above me.

"Left Hand of Darkness," I replied.

"Le Guin? You don't seem like a sci-fi person," the stranger said.

I laughed. "What kind of person do I seem like then?"

He gestured the spot next to me. I patted the ground, telling him to sit down. He sat down gracefully.

"You look like a man who reads business books. You now, the type of man who works at a holding as a CEO,"

"I am flattered," I said sarcastically.

He laughed. Two dimples appeared when his laugh ceased into a smile.

"What's your name?" I asked.

"Alex," he held out his hand, "Alexander William McKenzie,"

"Aidan Brown," I shook his hand.

"Nice to meet you," he said, his hand lingered on mine for a minute.

Alex was a ginger with pale skin and green eyes. He had a slim body. Despite that, he looked charming. We talked on the beach for another hour or so when Elisa came back. She looked angry.

"Who is this?" she barked.

Alex stood up and held his hand out to Elisa, "I'm Alex,"

Elisa looked at his hand with disgust and turned to me, "I'm going to our room, honey," she said.

"Okay," I murmured. She clearly expected me to go with her, but I was having fun, "I'll stay a bit more,"

"She is… Uhm, intense?" said Alex.

"Yes, she doesn't like me talking to strangers," I sighed.

"Then I have to become familiar with you," he said and put his hand on my leg.

I looked at him. His eyes were grassy, and they lured me towards him. I felt an urge within me, a call to lay beneath him and let him take me. I shook my head.

"Do you want to go grab something to eat?" he asked lively.

I nodded.

We sat down at a table with our food. Deep down, I knew Elisa was waiting for me, but I did not want to leave Alex. He made me felt at ease.

"So, Aidan," he started, "What else do you like?"

"Well, I am a linguist," I said, "I love languages. Also, I like sci-fi and fantasy novels,"

"Interesting. What else?"

"I am a huge Lord of the Rings fan," I admitted, my face turned pink.

"You got to be kidding me!" exclaimed Alex.

"No?" I replied.

"I love Lord of the Rings too," he laughed, "Which book is your favorite?"

"The Fellowship of the Ring, but when it comes to the films, I prefer the Return of the King," I explained.

"Oh, my God! Me too!" he smiled, "I knew we'd click when I was approaching you,"

"I am glad you did. However, I must go now,"

"Okay, my room number is 666. If you want to visit, my door is open to you.

When I returned to our room, Elisa was waiting for me. She was frowning. She turned her head sharply and glared at me.

"I am not in the mood, El," I said.

"Oh, really? Our little, wounded boy is not in the mood?"

"El," my voice was filled with warning.

"Don't you think I'd want my husband to be with me on our honeymoon?" she cried out.

"Well, I could ask the same! The way you flirted with Kai was disgusting!"

"Oh, so now we're jealous?" She laughed hysterically.

"I can't deal with you right now," I got out of the room.

I did not know where I should go, but my feet took me to the place I needed the most.

CHAPTER 4

I was standing in front of room number 666. I had raised my hand to knock when the door opened. A steady hand pulled me in and slammed the door shut. I saw a glimpse of green eyes before getting slammed to the closest wall.

It was Alex, but he was different. His breath was brushing my neck when he whispered:

"Tell me you came here to have sex,"

His voice was full of need. He pushed himself to me, and I felt him. He was bigger than me. I swallowed loudly. He pulled his face back to face me. His face was perfect with his straight nose and plump lips. His eyes were big and bright, and his lashes were light-colored, nearly blonde. He was taller than me, but still, he was looking at me from under his lashes. I realized he was holding onto me. He bit his lips and looked at me, begging with nothing but his perfect green eyes. I wanted to give in. To give in and kiss him was all I wanted now. I never lived my life with my emotions in control. I wanted to try that for a day. I leaned in and kissed him.

"He was waiting for this," I thought.

He held my arms above my head and deepened the kiss. He slid his tongue in my mouth, and I thought how brilliant he was as a kisser. His lips were like clouds. Soft and sweet. I could still taste the desert he had at lunch. Chocolate pudding. I kissed him more passionately. I wanted him.

"I want you too," he groaned into my mouth.

I chuckled to my idiotic self. Alex smiled into the kiss and pulled his shirt off, tossed it to the ground. I touched him, afraid of this being a dream. I never felt like this before. This was intense.

His chest was covered in thin, ginger hair. I like the way it felt under my hands. I touched his arm, his neck. His skin was smooth.

I parted from the kiss and started kissing his jaw. Tracing his jawline, I went down to his neck. His Adam's apple was moving underneath my lips as I sucked it. Alex groaned. It sounded heavenly. What was happening to me? I felt my penis get harder than ever.

"I know this isn't the best time, but I don't want you to regret anything," Alex whispered.

I pulled back to look at him, "What?"

"I know you're married, but you seemed so sad when she was around," he explained.

I looked down. Alex grabbed my chin and raised my head to face him. His eyes were soft, and his touch was softer, as if I were something that could break within his hands.

"I don't want you to regret anything."

Words echoed in my mind. I thought about Elisa and Kai and the unbearable question I could not ask. Would it break me if I do something that makes me happy? Would it be wrong to surrender to my feelings? Would it be wrong to want to be happy? No, it would not. I deserved to be happy.

I looked at Alex.

"I won't," I said and leaned in for a soft kiss.

He pulled himself back, "What about your wife?" he asked.

"I will have a divorce anyway," I said coldly, "I don't love her, and I believe she cheated on me first." I laughed.

Alex leaned towards me, "If you still have strength when I am done with you, we will talk about this," he whispered and kissed me before I could refuse.

As his tongue wandered inside my mouth, I gave in to him. I moaned his name. He laughed and pushed his body to mine. His mouth left mine and went down to my neck, sucking and leaving small marks of this sinful act.

His hand soon found their way to the end of my shirt and pulled it off me. As his mouth kept wondering my upper body, he pulled down my shorts. I was, now, as naked as a baby in front of him. My penis stood erect, waiting, no, yearning for the smallest touch.

"Touch me," I managed to whisper.

"Not yet," Alex replied. He was working on my collarbone.

His hands were circling my nipples, and I found out it felt good to be touched like that. It felt divine, like this was what this should feel like. There was no pressure, no rush. It was just us, our bodies close to one another, his lips on my collarbone.

He stopped and looked up to my face. He smiled.

"You look beautiful when you're blushed," he said, reaching for my lips once again, 'Now I will give you the thing you want."

He held my hand and guided me to bed. I sat down, feeling a little shy. Alex kneeled in front of me. I swallowed hard. He looked up, smiled, and took my tip in his mouth. My head fell back, and I groaned.

"Oh, that's so good,"

Alex chuckled and went deeper. I closed my eyes shut in pleasure. I could feel his tongue swirling around my tip.

"A-Alex!" I exclaimed, reaching a sudden climax.

Alex did not pull out. I heard him swallow all of it. As he stood up, I saw my penis was still hard. I looked at him.

"Don't worry. I am not done with you," he smirked.

I bit my lower lip in when he got rid of his shorts. He looked like an ancient Greek God's sculpture with his gorgeous naked body. I felt my penis harden even more.

"Someone looks ready?" he smirked.

I smiled back, unsure.

"Are you a top or a bottom?" he asked.

"I don't know. I have never done this before," I replied.

"Okay, uhm… How does the bottom sound like? It is easier, and if it hurts too much we can switch,"

"But what about you?" I asked.

"I am a switch, and I can do both easily," he answered.

I nodded. Alex climbed on top of me and pushed me back to the bed. He gave me a soft kiss and traced his way down to my crotch. As he cared for my penis, he pushed two of his fingers into my mouth. I sucked. He pulled them out when they were wet enough and slid one finger into me. I gasped.

"I'm sorry," he murmured but didn't pull out, "It will get better soon," he said, as he slid the second finger in.

It felt like nothing I have ever known. It was intense and painful. Alex pulled out his fingers and looked at me.

"I think you're ready," he said softly, "Tell me if it hurts too much,"

I nodded. He positioned himself on me and slowly slid in. I felt as if something was tearing apart inside me. It was painful. I closed my eyes shut and waited for him to move. He did not. I opened one of my eyes to look at him. He was looking at me. I kissed him gently and reassuringly. He lightly moaned as he started to move.

He was slow, as though he was afraid to hurt me. His lips were wandering around my neck smoothly, kissing and sucking.

"You are so tight," he groaned.

"Thanks?" I said, chuckling.

He laughed. His laugh was beautiful, and it made me forget the pain.

"Do you think you're ready for me to move faster?" he asked.

"I am," I said more confidently than I felt.

Alex smirked and moved. I gasped, but this time from pleasure. That intense pleasure came back and filled the place of pain.

I felt the rise inside me. I was close.

"I am close," Alex groaned, getting faster with every thrust.

"Me too," I moaned.

He thrust deeper. And as he hit a particular spot, we both reached climax. I felt a warmth on our bellies. Alex collapsed on me, and I felt how heavy my actions felt. I closed my eyes and, without a single doubt, fell into a chaotic sleep.

"Yes, Matthew, harder! Fuck me harder!"

I heard voices in the void. There was a door in front of me. White and sleek. It looked like my mother's bedroom door. I pushed open the door and saw them: My mother and uncle Matthew. He was on top of my naked mother and doing something that looked painful. They did not notice me, so I slowly backed away. My eyes were locked on my screaming mother.

I was still looking at them when the floor slipped underneath me. I started falling. I wondered if Alice felt like this when she was falling down the rabbit hole.

As I fell, I saw images forming around me. The day I met Elisa was on my right, and the first time I kissed William was on my left. I felt as though I was reliving all these memories. When I managed to look down, I saw a blinding light at the end of this hole. I got closer and closer, and with every passing second, I felt more. It started to overwhelm me. As I felt tears rolling down my eyes, I wished this to stop. I wanted to shout out for help, but I could not find my voice. Around me, more and more memories formed.

The moving in. The proposal. The wedding. The graduation. My father's death. The funeral. Meeting Kai. Meeting Alex.

Alex... the mere thought of him, calmed me down. I was closer to the light now. I reached out to it, and everything turned white.

When I got my vision back, I was at a beach. There was only a man sitting on the sand and me. I walked towards the man. As I got closer, I recognized the familiar face.

"Father?" I asked.

The man turned his face to me. With the sight, I put my hand over my mouth, trying not to vomit. The other half of the man's face was rotten. There were worms eating the dead flesh. There was no eye in its place; instead, I could see a void like the one I came from.

"You will pay like I did, son," the man said.

His voice sent chills down my spine.

"Pay for what?" I asked, fearing the answer would be about Alex.

"For marrying a woman, you don't love," the man looked to the ocean, "My time has come," he turned back to me.

I pursed my lips and tried not to look at the rotten half. I heard screams coming from somewhere close. Agonizing screams… they sounded like someone was getting tortured. I looked around me for a source. It was easy to find; there were people bounded to the waves. They were getting torn apart, leaving red marks on the water. I swallowed.

"Are you going back there?" I asked the man.

"Yes," he said without looking at me, "I have to pay for my mistakes,"

I opened my eyes in terror. Someone held me down. It was not Elisa. She was not strong enough. I looked around only to see Alex. He looked worried.

"Are you alright?" he asked, putting his arm around me, "You're safe, it was just a nightmare,"

His voice was soothing. I relaxed into his arms. Then I remembered the man's words.

"You will pay for marrying a woman you don't love,"

"Want to talk about it?" Alex asked.

I shook my head.

"I… I have to go, Alex," I said, getting out of the bed.

"Okay?" he said.

I sensed a sadness within his voice. I kissed him.

"Give me your phone," I murmured. He obeyed. I typed my number and saved it.

"If you ever come around Cambridge, Massachusetts, hit me up," I winked.

"But your wife?"

"What wife?" I laughed, "I will be a divorced man,"

I finished getting dressed and kissed him one last time. I left the room 666 with one thought in my mind: I must get a divorce as soon as possible.

CHAPTER 5

I came back to an empty room. I could see the phantoms of us, but there was no real person.

"It's better," I thought.

I sat down on the table, pulled out a pen and a piece of paper. I was a logical person and wanted to make a pro-con chart. Everything I thought would benefit me from a divorce was written on the right, and everything would not help me were on the left. When I was done, the left side overcame the right side. The path I had to choose was, once again, evident.

The door opened, and the woman I once loved came in. The moment she saw me, all life drained from her face.

"What's wrong, baby?" said another male voice.

It was Kai… He came into the room to see me, sitting on the chair like a sculpture, motionless. No one spoke for a moment.

"I have to go," said Kai and left without a second glance.

We were alone in the room. The silence between us was so sharp that it could cut anything. I waited for the first words to fell as if waiting for a bomb to go off.

Elisa cleared her throat. "I know, saying, "It is not what you think," won't change anything, so, um…"

"I want a divorce," I said, cutting her off.

"What?" she whispered.

"You heard me," I said.

"Aiden, I am so sorry. Please forgive me!" she cried, kneeling in front of me.

"It's not what I saw," I turned my head away from her.

I did not want to tell her that I did not love her. So, I told a different reason.

"I slept with another person,"

The shock in Elisa's face was almost unbearable, but almost.

"You did what?" she whispered.

"You heard me," I said calmly.

She stood up, back down, and sat down on the bed. After a minute of intense silence, she started laughing hysterically. I could see tears forming in her eyes.

"Well," she said, "At least I don't have to live with the fact that I slept with another person too."

"This isn't your first time doing it," I said.

"How do you know that?" she asked, looking a bit annoyed.

"I saw the way you came back to the hotel the day we went to the city tour."

"Oh…"

"Look, Elisa, I loved you madly once, but that love had faded away. I cannot live my life with a person I do not love. Especially when they cheated on me on multiple occasions," I explained.

She looked at me, "Was she better than me?" she asked simply.

I doubted but then decided to be honest, "He was,"

"He?" she was startled, "You cheated on me with a man?"

I swallowed, "Yes," I admitted.

The pain of my cheek was so sudden and unexpected that my face turned to the side. My hand touched my burning, probably red, cheek. I looked at Elisa as she cried. There was no way I could imagine how she must have felt. She backed off and started to pack. I watched as she clumsily put her things into her luggage. This was our fault. We should never have married in the first place.

The next time I saw her was at the airport. She was checking in. I approached her cautiously.

"Elisa?"

"What do you want?" she asked without looking at my face.

"Here," I pass her a bunch of signed papers, "The moment you sign these, we will have no other connection left. And do not worry, the written reason is my adultery," I said, trying to comfort her a bit.

She took the papers and pulled out a pen. I watched as she signed the divorce papers, gave them back, and raised her head to face me. She looked as though tears were pricking her eyes. She was obviously in pain.

"Goodbye, Aiden," she said with a cracked voice.

I nodded. She turned around and left. I did not see her on the plane.

CHAPTER 6

"Class dismissed. Don't forget your assignments for next week,"

I watched as the students leave the hall. It has been two years since I saw Elisa, and somewhere deep down, I was starting to regret it. After that week in that Caribbean island, I did not hear of Alex. The thought of him seeing me as a one-night stand broke my heart at first, but I got used to it.

I was walking down the corridors of MIT when I saw him again. William. He was there talking to a student of mine. The student was showing what seemed like the way of my classroom. William looked at my direction, and the student showed me. Our eyes locked, and he waved at me. I waved back. He ran toward me like in the old days. He seemed childish, like always.

"Aidan! How are you?" he asked. His voice was deeper than I remembered.

"William, I am fine. What about you? You have changed since last saw each other!" I replied.

"Well, that was six years ago when you dumped me for a bitch. But tell me, I heard you got a divorce after a week. What happened?"

"It's a long story," I said, "Why don't you come to my place for dinner and find out about it?" I winked.

"Of course, Mr. Linguist at MIT," he replied jokingly.

"Here's my number," I gave him the numbers and told him to text me later.

"I'll see you at 7 pm sharp," I added.

"Yes, Sir," he shouted.

We laughed, and I left him there to go home. On my way home, I remembered all our memories. He was my first kiss and my best friend. I wondered why I never got back in touch with him.

The bonfire was the only light in the pitch-black night. I did not know what time it was. All I knew was William, my best friend, was on top of me.

How did we come to this? Oh, right! I tried to take his letter, and we struggled, then he climbed on top of me. Now, he was staring at my parted lips with hunger. He switched his gaze to my eyes. I was in shock. All I knew was that I wanted to be kissed.

We were going to an all-boys boarding school, and I was not good with girls. I raised my head a bit, and he lowered his. Our lips brushed each other. I felt something hardened in my uniform, so did William. He smirked and touched it. My back arched.

He leaned in and kissed me properly this time. It was like in the movies except we were the teenage boys. He parted from me. I saw him lick his lips as he sat down.

There was a bulge in his trousers too. He pulled me on top of him and made me sat on his lap. As I wrapped my legs to his body, I kissed him.

His lips were soft. Now I understood why he was using chapstick all the time. There was a small peppermint taste to them, but I could taste the dinner's dessert. William turned his head to the side and pushed his tongue into my mouth. I moaned. This was good.

I felt his hands on my hips. Eagerly, I pushed myself towards his body; I wanted more. But he parted from me.

"This was fun," he said, as if this was something he did often.

"You're different from other boys, Aidan. How can I say? More... innocent," he added.

I was more innocent, and I felt used. He did this with other boys too.

"How come I never knew about them?" I asked,

He laughed at this question, "Well, I don't have to share everything with you now, do I?"

I nodded, but there was something that made me sick. I did not know what it was, so I let it go.

Looking back, now, I understood most of my emotions. I used to like William, and what I felt was jealousy. I wondered if inviting him over dinner was a mistake. I shook my head. It was too late to regret it now.

Throughout the dinner, we talked about what happened since the last time we saw each other. William was studying Law at university. Now he was a well-known lawyer. He had a couple of relationships with both genders but nothing serious. I told him about how I fell out of love with Elisa and that she cheated on me. I excluded Alex from these stories. He was for me only.

After dinner, we opened a bottle of wine and sat in front of the TV. I caught a few lustful looks as we sat down and talked.

"So, Elisa cheated on you two years ago. Do you have anyone else in your life right now?" he said sort of seductively.

"Nope," I replied as I refilled my glass and took a sip.

"That's long," he whispered.

"Yep," I said and finished my glass.

I looked at him, only to find him already looking at me. He put his glass down.

"You know," he said as he sat closer to me, "I've always liked you."

"How many glasses you had?" I asked, laughing.

"I dunno," he made a hiccup.

"Okay, big boy. You are drunk,"

"No, I am not." He said putting his head to my shoulder, "Even if I am, I still know what I want,"

"Oh, really?" I said sarcastically, "Tell me then,"

"*You*,"

My smile faded away. For two long years, I imagined one person and acted on the phantom of one specific occasion. Was I ready to move on?

William was leaving small kisses on my neck. I turned my neck to the other side to give him more space.

"That's my boy," he murmured.

I moaned. His touch was soft, like the day we made out. But this time we were adults, and we could do so much more. I remembered the bulge underneath me, how big it was when he was 16.

"B-bedroom…" I said faintly.

"Show me the way," he whispered onto my skin.

I stood up and held will's hand. He kept touching me as I led him to my bedroom, where I slept alone for the last two years.

When we passed through the door, he turned me around and pushed me to the bed. I was caught off guard, and I fell back. As he took his shirt slowly, I got rid of my shirt and stood on my elbows. I had seen him naked before… when we were 16. His body had changed a lot. He had abs now, and his shoulders were broader. He bent over and pulled my trousers and boxer off. I was left naked in front of him. He got rid of his jeans and boxers too and climbed on top of me.

He started jerking me as his mouth left marks all over my chest. He kneeled in front of the bed and moaned.

"Oh, how I wanted to do this back when we were younger," he took my penis into his mouth and moaned.

He was good at *that*, like good. I groaned his name in pleasure over and over before climaxing into his mouth. He swallowed and looked up to me.

"Turn around," he demanded.

I obeyed. He positioned himself to my entrance. As he got in, I cried out loud in pain.

"I'm sorry. Do you have lube?" he asked.

I shook my head. I did not even touch myself properly.

"It's okay. I can take it," I said but gasped when he moved.

"I know a solution," he said, and moments later, I felt something wet back there.

Was he licking me? I tried to look back, but he positioned me back.

"Stay still," he ordered. I obeyed.

The wetness made me relax. A minute later, he slid inside me easily.

"Oh, yes," I moaned.

"You are tighter than I imagined," he commented.

I did not say anything. Instead, I closed my eyes and enjoyed myself. The way he moved in me made memories flash in my mind.

Alex… he was so much better than William. So much more intimate. What I felt with him was different. I wanted him. I missed him. Yet there I was getting fucked by my old best friend.

I did not open my eyes until William climaxed inside me. I swallowed and turned around.

"You didn't like it? Oh my God, were you a top?" he asked, horrified.

"No and no," I answered.

"Then why are you looking sad?"

"I will tell you, but first, I need a shower," I walked to the bathroom, naked.

After the shower, I found William asleep in my bed. I laid next to him and fell into another chaotic sleep.

I woke up the next morning with the clattering coming from the kitchen. I got out of the bed and headed towards the kitchen only to see William in his underwear, making breakfast.

"The sleepyhead woke up finally," he said jokingly.

I smiled but said nothing. He gestured the kitchen table, and I sat down. The meal looked delicious. There were scrambled eggs and bacon, some greens, and orange juice.

"Start eating." William said flipping a pancake on the pan, "The pancakes will be ready soon,"

After breakfast, we sat in the living room, talking. I was trying to avoid talking about last night.

"Who is Alex?" William asked.

"What?" I asked, eyes widened. How did he know?

"You moaned his name all night in your sleep," he explained, "So, who is Alex?"

I looked down. Who was Alex to me, really?

"He is the first man I slept with," I said.

"Well, he definitely left some trouble behind," he said, not looking to my face.

"Yes," I answered.

Alex left a wound in my heart that never healed. I never thought about it till now, but I really liked him. William looked at me and slowly leaned in. I kissed him to numb the pain, and he knew. I gave in to William and tried to forget Alex.

William stayed for a week. Every night I tried to numb the pain of regret. I should never have left him there. I should have done something. I knew this thinking would not help my situation, but overthinking was all I could do.

After William left, I got worse. I turned to various things to numb the pain: alcohol, sex, speeding, etc. Until one day.

It started with my usual headache. I got dressed as I swallowed two painkillers. My routine did not have breakfast anymore. I did not know what laid ahead of me. All I knew was that I needed Alex.

CHAPTER 7

It was a regular day, or so I thought. I had no idea what was about to happen when I get to the campus. As I walked down the corridors, I saw a glimpse of bright red. I turned around, but nothing was there.

"Looking for someone?" a familiar voice echoed in the empty corridor.

I looked around. Over the corner stood Alex, grinning exactly how I remembered.

"Alex," I breathed and ran to him.

He opened his arms and took me in his embrace. I buried my head to his neck and took a deep breath. After all these years, he smelled the same.

"I missed you," he whispered.

With the voice coming from the other end of the corridor, we parted.

"What are you doing here?" I asked.

"I told you. I missed you," he answered.

"Mr. Brown?" a student called my name.

We both turned our heads to her.

"I am coming right away," I said.

"Go," Alex said, sticking a paper in my hand, "I'll see you tonight." He placed a quick kiss on my lips when no one was looking and left.

I was standing there, smiling like an idiot. I looked at the paper. It was the address of my favorite restaurant.

"He remembered," I whispered to myself.

The day flew by. When I was getting ready at home, I could not recall half of what I did throughout the day. I decided on white shirt and black trousers. I combed my hair and put-on cologne. When I was done getting ready, I realized I still had an hour. I groaned in frustration. The whole day flew by, but the last 2 hours were like two decades.

I decided to walk to the restaurant instead of going by car. That would waste some time. I put on my earbuds and played a soft, romantic jazz song. As I walked to the restaurant, I hummed the lyrics from under my breath.

When I arrived at the place, I realized it was closed. I was confused, and it was only 7 pm. I saw Henry, the owner, inside. I knocked on the glass.

"Henry, what's going on?" I asked.

"A young man rented the whole place for the night. I'm sorry, Aidan, but you have to come another time," he replied and went back inside.

I turned around and sat on the pavement. Our night was ruined. Like there was no way Alex could rent the place. I pulled out my phone and started searching for other locations nearby.

"Why are you sitting on the pavement?"

"Alex!" I stood up and hugged him.

"Are you alright?" he asked.

"Yes- err… No, someone rent out the whole place. I was looking for alternatives, but there is no use. All the good places ask for a reservation. And…" he stopped me by kissing me.

"Aidan, I am the one who rented the place."

My mouth fell open. He did what?

"Shall we go in?" he asked, putting a hand on my waist.

I nodded. We got in.

I have never seen this place like this before. There were candles everywhere, and the music was so much more romantic than usual. I looked to my side, and Alex was there. It was like a dream come true. There were no tables to be seen except one. Right in the middle of the room, for two. The hand on my waist led me towards the table and pulled the chair back for me. I sat down, and Alex sat in front of me.

"I already ordered your favorite," he explained when Henry brought homemade tomato soups.

"After all this time, why now?" I asked, sipping from my soup.

"Well, I tried to forget you," he started, "But I failed miserably, all this time you were in my mind and I finally managed to get a job offer here. If you think we can work out, I will accept it,"

I was stunned.

"Alex, I- I don't know what to say," I stuttered.

"Say you'll think about it," he said, holding my hand.

"I will think about it,"

"Good," he said with a wide smile, "Now, let us talk of other stuff. What have you done for the past two years?"

I looked away, not wanting him to know about William.

"I know about the other guy. But I thought he was not serious," he said.

I looked up, "How?"

"I saw you two kissing a couple of weeks ago. And yes, I was stalking you," he bit inside his mouth visibly and looking away.

I laughed, "His name is William. He used to be my best friend, and we hooked up a few times. He left for New York, though," the tension was gone.

"That's good," he said.

"Why?" I asked, smirking.

"Well," he stopped, "I want you to myself only," he murmured.

"I couldn't hear you," I said, my voice filled with mischief.

He leaned on the table and hissed, "If you don't want to get fucked in the bathroom shut up," I could see the mischievous little boy in his eyes.

"You wouldn't dare," I said, leaning forward.

"Wanna bet?" he asked, raising one red eyebrow.

I leaned back suddenly, "No,"

We talked about anything and everything after that. He was an artist, so he was having lots of commission in the USA. That was another reason to move, but he said the main reason was me. When the dessert came, I moaned.

"Oh, I love this one,"

"I know," he laughed, "You told me the whole menu when we first met,"

"I did, right!" I said, "Do you think it is as good as I told you about?"

"Yes, but you're better." He winked.

I felt the blood rushing to my ears and cheeks. Alex laughed.

"You're blushing!"

I closed my face with my hands. He reached out and took my hand off my face.

"I love it when you blush," he whispered softly and added, "Why don't we get the dessert for take out and go to your place?"

I nodded. Alex showed me the way to his car after we got the dessert.

The car journey was silent except me giving direction to him. When we arrived, I took out my keys.

I was about to open the door when I felt a hand on my hip. I dropped the keys and bent over to get them. My hips brushed against Alex's crotch, and I felt the big bulge in his jeans. He was hard already, and I knew the night was going to be longer than usual.

We got in. I showed him the kitchen, and he put the dessert in the fridge. I was close to him, so I took advantage of this and kissed his neck. He paused. I thought I did something wrong.

"Someone wants to be a bad boy, huh?" he asked, turned, and pushed me backward. I put my hand on the counter and sat on top of it. He came closer between my legs. I wrapped them around his waist and put my hands on his neck. He leaned in, kissed me.

I let out a loud moan. It was always different with him. Always more intense. I kissed him back. As our tongues tasted each Alex groaned. His hands were all around me, like he could not get enough of me. He pushed his body to mine.

"Oh, how much I have missed you," he moaned.

"I missed you too," I said.

I shut my eyes as his mouth wandered on my neck, leaving love marks. It was too good. I could feel my penis pushing the fabric of my clothes. It was throbbing with lust and passion. I wanted to have him inside me.

"I want you, Alex," I groaned.

"You have to wait," he chuckled, "also I don't know where the bedroom is,"

"I want you to take me here. Forget the bedroom," I said, my eyes still closed.

Alex backed off and took his jeans and underwear off. He was already erect enough. I looked at him. He was looking at me, asking if it is alright. I pulled him into a kiss. That was enough for him. He ripped my shirt with one move and tossed it to the marble ground. I hopped down from the counter and got rid of my trousers. Alex raised me up and sat me back down to the bar. As he sucked the sensitive skin over my collarbone, he pushed two fingers into my mouth to make them wet. I sucked eagerly.

When they were ready, he started to finger me. One finger first, then the second. When I was stretched enough, he positioned himself to my entrance and pushed it in. As I took him all the way in, we both moaned. He started to move, and I realized it did not hurt when it was him. Not because he was smaller but because I wanted him more. He moved in me as if he wanted this for year. And maybe, I thought, he did want *this* for years.

As our bodies tangled, I felt at peace, at home. His every movement was in sync with mine, and we were not even trying for that. We were one but separated at the same time. We were like two sides of a coin: completely different, yet one in its' core. I felt divinity in me when we both reached climax.

Alex's breath was brushing against my neck. It was shallow but fast. He swallowed.

"I can't find the words to describe how many times I dreamed of this," he whispered.

"Try," I said, as he pulled out and helped me get down from the counter.

"Let's take the dessert then," he smiled.

We got dressed and sat on the couch with our desserts. He started to tell me what he had done all this time. He went back to Scotland two days after me. He was a psychology student back then, and now, he was an EMDR therapist.

"What about love life?" I asked.

"Well, I tried to have some relationships, but I kept seeing your face, to be honest," he said.

My jaw dropped, "Me too!" I exclaimed.

He looked at me in shock. I blushed, realizing how silly I must have looked.

"Are you blushing?" he raised my head to face him.

"I was silly," I admitted.

Alex let out a laugh, "I thought you were cute," his face saddened a bit, "Though I was a bit jealous also."

"Jealous?"

"Yeah, I mean, it is stupid, but I wanted to be the only guy you, you know…"

I placed an innocent kiss on his cheek, "You were my first, and I want you to be my last."

"Really?" he was surprised by my words.

"Yes, so maybe you should consider taking that job you were talking about," I winked.

He gave me a passionate kiss. As our tongues touched, I moaned loudly. Alex broke the kiss.

"Where is the bedroom?" he asked.

"Second left door in the corridor," I whispered, my eyes half-closed.

Alex kissed me and lifted me up. I wrapped my legs around his waist. The next thing I remembered was him lowering me to a soft ground. I was on my bed, and he was on me, leaving marks all around my neck.

He drew his way to my collarbone and started to suck. I touched his crotch and felt his penis on my hand. It was stiff as hell. The way he fit into my hand was amazing. It was like his body was made to be mine.

Alex drew back and looked down at me. Mostly at the place he sucked. It must have turned into a dark purple color. He switched his gaze on mine.

"I am so fortunate," he said, as if he was talking to himself.

I wanted to ask why, but I did not. I knew he was not going to be honest with me. Not at that moment, at least. So, I raised my body to kiss him. We were in harmony. The way we kissed way divine-like. At that moment, there were only us in the whole universe. Us and our bodies.

We parted, trying to catch our breaths. I started tugging on his shirt, and he laughed at my neediness. As an answer, I began to undo his shirt, and when I am done, I got rid of mine. Alex stopped me halfway through.

"I'll do the rest," his voice was firm and confident.

He laid me down and began to undo the rest of my buttons.

Again, I felt the universe revolving around us. Every star every planet and galaxy were turning around us. We were like Gods creating divinity.

Alex undid my pants and pulled them down. I tilted on my place to help him. I was free of any earthly materials. He got rid of his and lid next to me, his face facing mine. I kissed him. He deepened the kiss. Our tongues twisted together, and it felt like creating galaxies.

I climbed on top of him and kept kissing him like it was all I could. I let his taste merge with mine, second by second. He tasted like a combination of chocolate and mint. That taste was grounding. Without it, I would lose my mind. I led his penis to my entrance and slowly slid it inside. We both moaned as I took him in.

I started to move. His hands grasped my hips and led the way. We did not part our lips. It was as if he, too, was afraid of losing his sanity.

I felt my stomach twist with pleasure as he hit my sweet spot.

"Alex," I groaned.

"Aidan!" Alex whispered heavily, "Fuck, I am…"

I felt his warmth inside me. That was my limit. I climaxed as he pushed himself deep inside me one last time.

"A-Alex!"

Our bodies descended from heavenly skies and softened as we caught our breaths.

"So, should I accept the offer?" Alex asked softly.

My face was buried in his neck. I nodded.

"Yes, please,"

He looked at me and smiled.

I turned my head to the side, and as sleep took over, I thought to myself:

"I won't pay like you did, father."

THE END